Princess
Katie's
Kittens

Princess Katie's Kittens

Collect all the kittens!

Pixie at the Palace
Bella at the Ball

☆

Coming Soon:

Poppy and the Prince
Suki in the Snow
Tilly and the Tiara
Pebbles and the Puppy

Julie Sykes

Princess Katie's Kittens

Bella at the Ball

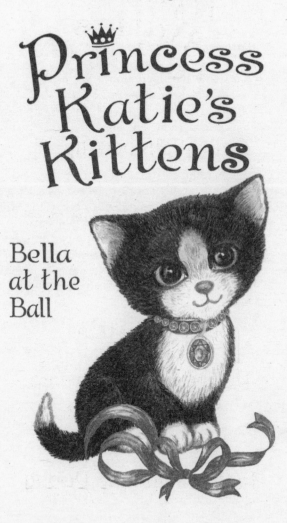

PICCADILLY PRESS • LONDON

For Joanne and Claire

First published in Great Britain in 2012
by Piccadilly Press Ltd,
5 Castle Road, London NW1 8PR
www.piccadillypress.co.uk

A catalogue record for this book is available
from the British Library

ISBN: 978 1 84812 239 0 (paperback)

1 3 5 7 9 10 8 6 4 2

Printed and bound by CPI Group (UK) Ltd,
Croydon, CR0 4YY
Cover design by Simon Davis
Cover illustration by Sue Hellard
Inside illustrations by Richard Morgan

Chapter 1

A Toy Mouse

Princess Katie of Tula and her best friend Becky Philips hurried along the palace corridor towards the boot room. They were on their way to see Princess Katie's kittens. It had been a whole week since Katie had found the six tiny cats abandoned in a box in the woods, and Becky had helped her to rescue them.

'Hello, kitties!' called Katie, pushing open the boot room door.

Immediately, Pixie, the silver grey tabby, stopped attacking the laces of the king's walking boots and pranced over. He weaved round Katie's legs, rubbing his head against her.

Katie scratched him under the chin. Pixie purred ecstatically, then suddenly a black and white ball of fluff cannoned into him, knocking him over.

'Bella, really you are a cheeky thing!' Katie exclaimed.

Pixie sprang up and cuffed Bella with a paw. Bella batted him back and the two kittens rolled together on the floor.

'It's a good thing we don't play like that,' giggled Becky.

'Can you imagine what Dad would say?' Katie agreed. She made her voice go deep like the king's. 'Princesses *never* fight.'

Becky dug into her pocket and pulled out a felt mouse with a long string tail. The mouse jingled as Becky showed it to Katie.

'Look what Mum bought for the kittens. It's got a bell inside and it smells of catnip, which cats love.'

Becky put the mouse on the floor and pulled its long string. The mouse wiggled towards her. It looked so real that for a second Katie thought it had moved by itself. Immediately, Bella and Pixie stopped fighting and stared at the tinkling mouse. Then Bella pounced. But Becky was too quick, pulling the mouse just out of her reach.

'Look at her little face!' Katie couldn't stop laughing. Bella was so surprised. She crouched down, ears pricked, whiskers twitching. Her fluffy black tail stretched out behind her as she bunched her body and sprang at the mouse again.

'Missed!' Becky chuckled, pulling it out of her reach.

Soon it wasn't just Bella chasing the toy mouse. Pixie and Poppy joined in too. Sometimes Becky let one of the kittens catch it, but not too often. It was more fun watching them skitter around after it.

'This is fun,' said Katie, when it was her turn to work the mouse. She lifted it off the ground, making the kittens jump in the air for it.

Katie was enjoying herself so much that she totally forgot about the time. It wasn't until the queen poked her head around the door that she remembered she had a dress fitting. It was Mum's birthday very soon and the king was holding a special birthday ball to celebrate. Katie was going to perform a dance for the queen in front of all of the guests and she was having a dress made especially for the occasion. Her heart missed a beat. Would Mum be cross with her?

'Sorry, Mum,' she said, handing the mouse to Becky and leaping to her feet.

The queen smiled. 'It's all right, darling. You're not late yet. Have you seen Alfie? He's having a new suit too.'

Alfie was Katie's little brother. He was often a noisy nuisance, but he looked up to his big sister and they mostly got on well together.

'Why is Alfie having a new suit?' asked

Katie. 'I thought he was too young to go to the ball.'

'He is, but your father has agreed that he can come and see you dance.'

'Oh!' Katie's stomach fluttered nervously. She hoped Alfie would behave himself and not put her off!

Becky tucked the mouse back in her jeans pocket.

'I'd better go. Mum's been busy getting things ready for the ball and I promised her I'd help get the tea tonight.'

Mrs Philips was the housekeeper at

Starlight Palace and the family lived in an apartment in the palace's west tower.

Hurriedly, Katie and Becky said goodbye to the kittens. Bella caught hold of Katie's jeans and wouldn't let go.

'Sorry, Bella, but I don't have time to play any more.'

Katie needed Becky's help to gently pull Bella away from her leg. Bella chased the girls to the door, so Katie opened it a crack and let Becky squeeze out first, then followed herself. As the door shut Bella cried in disappointment.

'I'll be back soon, kitties!' called Katie.

'Good luck with the dress fitting,' said Becky.

'Thanks,' said Katie, thinking she'd need it. She loved having new dresses, but she wasn't so keen on having them specially made. It meant standing still for ages.

'See you tomorrow?' Katie asked.

'Definitely,' said Becky.

Bella the black-and-white kitten stared at the door in disbelief. Why had Katie and Becky left so suddenly? Weren't they having a great game together with the delicious smelling jingly mouse? Feeling disappointed and let down, she sat on her bottom, lifted one black leg and washed her white tummy. Next she cleaned her four white paws before starting on the rest of her body, finishing with her face. Daintily licking a paw, Bella wiped clean the white blaze down her nose, around her green eyes and head, and finally her coal-black ears.

That felt better! And what's more, now Bella had a plan. She would go and find the girls and see if they'd let her play with the jingly mouse again. But how was she going to get out? Katie had pulled on the handle halfway up, but that was far too high for Bella to reach. As she stood wondering what to do next, the door opened and Alfie looked in.

'Katie? Oh, she must have gone to the fitting without me.' He rushed off down the corridor.

In his hurry, Alfie didn't shut the door properly.

Hardly able to believe her good fortune,

Bella slipped through it then hesitated, not sure which way to go. She sniffed the carpet. To her left it was heavy with old scents, but to her right it smelt flowery, like Katie.

'This way,' Bella said to herself, pleased with her cleverness.

Confidently, she set out along the corridor to find her friend.

Chapter 2

Ghost!

'Princess Katie, you can move now,' said Mrs Snippet, waving a handful of pins.

Katie let her breath out in a noisy whoosh of relief.

'I was scared you might prick me,' she said.

Mrs Snippet put the spare pins in a tin in

her sewing box and smiled at Katie.

'I've been dressmaking for fifty years and not pricked anyone yet. But I suppose there's always a first time, Princess.'

Katie grinned. 'Well, I hope it won't be on me. Is my dress nearly finished now?'

'Nearly, it's a bit loose so it needs taking in, and then there's the hem to do.'

Mrs Snippet pulled a measuring tape out of her pocket and slipped it around Katie's waist.

'Please don't make it too tight,' said Katie, worried that she might not be able to dance in it.

'Don't worry. You can try it on again when I've finished,' Mrs Snippet reassured her.

Katie relaxed and stole a look in the full-length mirror. Her dress was the prettiest one she'd ever owned. It was lilac, her favourite colour, with a scooped neck and tiny sleeves. It went in at the waist and had two skirts, a lilac one on top with a zigzag hem that showed off the sparkly pink skirt underneath. The dress was fastened at the back with a line of lilac and pink rose-shaped buttons and a matching rose at her waist. Katie was going to finish it off with sparkly tights and silver dancing shoes.

There was a knock at the door. 'Are you dressed?' called the queen.

'Yes, come on in,' Katie answered.

Alfie bounded into the room first. 'Wow!' he said, his eyes popping. 'Is that a real rose?'

'Don't touch,' said Katie, hastily stepping back. 'Are your hands clean?'

'Of course!' Alfie lunged for the rose at Katie's waist. 'Alfie! That's enough,' said the queen, sternly.

'Go and sit on that stool until it's your turn.'

Sticking his tongue out at Katie, Alfie sat on the stool.

Katie turned her back on him. 'How shall I wear my hair?' she asked. 'Up or down?'

The queen tilted her head on one side, as Katie twisted her long blond hair up into a bun.

'It looks lovely like that. Wear it up for the ball and I'll lend you my tiara. It'll help keep your hair in place when you're dancing.'

'Really?'

The tiara had been made for the queen to wear on her wedding day and was very special. Katie rushed forward and hugged her.

'Thank you. That'd be perfect!'

'Careful, Princess,' said Mrs Snippet. 'The

dress is still pinned. You can take it off now. Go through to the sewing room and I'll come and help you when I've written down these measurements.'

Katie went into the room next door. Mrs Snippet's sewing machine was on the table along with another sewing box stuffed full of needles, pins, scissors and reels of thread. There were several dressmakers' dummies modelling the outfits that Mrs Snippet was making for the ball.

Alfie's small green velvet suit, her dad's grey one, her mother's dress and an empty dummy that was for Katie's dress. The dummies didn't have heads and they made Katie giggle. There was something a bit spooky about them, especially the one wearing her mum's long ball gown. Mrs Snippet had covered the dress with a large white sheet so that the king didn't see it, as the queen wanted it to be a surprise. It made the dummy look like a ghost.

'There's no such thing as ghosts,' she said to herself, sensibly.

She started to undo the buttons on her dress. Then suddenly she heard a rustle.

What was that? Katie stared at the dummies. The sheet covering her mum's dress was twitching. An icy shiver ran up her spine. No, surely she was imagining things? Katie blinked and looked again. This time, the sheet billowed just like a ghost.

'Aaargh!' Katie wanted to run away but her feet seemed glued to the floor.

The sheet rose and fell again. Katie's heart was thudding so hard it hurt. Forcing her legs to work, she started to back away. Something small and black and white shot out from under the sheet then disappeared. Katie stared in disbelief as a pink nose appeared next.

'Oh no!' she groaned.

Walking forward she carefully lifted the sheet.

'Bella! What are you doing here?'

'Meow!' Bella stared at Katie with big green eyes then stalked into the open.

'Aaargghh!' shrieked Mrs Snippet, who had chosen that moment to come in. 'A cat! Shoo!' she added, flapping her hands. 'Shoo, shoo.'

'It's all right Mrs Snippet. I'll get her,' said Katie.

'Princess, stop! Think of the cat hairs. And claws! You'll snag your new dress.'

Mrs Snippet tutted crossly as she ushered Bella to the door.

Bella looked confused. Katie badly wanted to pick her up but she didn't dare.

'It's OK, Bella,' she called as Mrs Snippet guided the kitten back to the hall then shut the door on her.

'It's *not* OK!' huffed Mrs Snippet. 'I *never* want to see that kitten here again. If anything happens to your new dress then what will you wear to the ball?'

'Sorry,' said Katie, meekly. 'I promise I'll make sure Bella stays away.'

The moment Katie was back in her jeans and T-shirt, she raced out of the sewing room to find Bella. The little black and white kitten was waiting sadly outside the door. She meowed loudly when she saw Katie.

'Oh Bella!' said Katie, scooping her up

and pressing her cheek against Bella's silky fur. 'You have to keep out of Mrs Snippet's room.'

On the way to the boot room Katie bumped into the king.

'Hello, darling. How's my favourite princess today?' he asked.

'I'm fine thanks, Dad,' said Katie.

'And how's your dance coming along for the birthday ball?'

'Well, it's OK.'

'I hope it's better than OK!' the king smiled. 'I've promised the queen she's going to have the best birthday ball ever.'

Katie grinned. 'You say that every year.'

'But this year is *extra* special,' said the king. 'Your mother's been working very hard and she deserves a treat. Promise you won't let me down?'

'I promise.'

'That's my girl.' The king patted Katie's arm before going on his way.

Anxiously, Katie carried the wriggling

Bella to the boot room. The kitten was so lively. Katie hoped she could keep her out of trouble. It would be a disaster if Bella's playful ways spoilt Mum's birthday ball.

Chapter 3

Something Fishy

Bella loved to play. As well as the jingly mouse that smelt so good, the girls brought other toys. The scratching post was great fun. Bella loved running her claws down it. At the top of the post was a platform to sit on, which she hadn't managed to climb up to yet, but had fun trying. When she grew too frustrated, she batted at the ball hanging from the platform.

The tunnel was another favourite. It was dark inside and rustled when she walked through it. It was also a good place to hide. Bella had invented a game where she hid in the tunnel and pounced on the other kittens when they walked past.

But Bella's favourite games were the ones when Katie and Becky joined in. The girls were such fun, teasing her with the jingly mouse and rolling balls for her to chase. They brought cat treats with them too. The fishy ones were delicious!

One morning Katie came alone.

'Becky's gone shopping with her mum to buy a dress for the ball,' she explained.

Bella didn't understand and was disappointed when Katie didn't spend long with her. She'd been hoping for a game of chase the mouse! But, after feeding the kittens and giving them fresh water, Katie left saying, 'I'll come and play with you this afternoon. I'm riding Misty now and then I have an extra dance lesson.'

Bella wandered over to Pixie who was sunning himself by the window.

'Come and play with me,' she mewed.

Pixie yawned. 'Later, when I'm not so full of breakfast.'

Tortoiseshell Poppy was having a wash. One leg was in the air as she cleaned her tummy.

'Come and play,' said Bella, pouncing on her tail.

'I'm busy,' purred Poppy.

The other kittens were curled up together in the basket. None of them wanted to play with Bella either. Half-heartedly, Bella batted a ball around. Her hitting grew harder and harder until the ball

rolled into the wall and bounced back at her. That was fun! Bella kept hitting the ball to see how far she could bounce it off the wall.

'Ouch!' squeaked Poppy loudly, as the ball accidently hit her on the nose.

'Sorry,' said Bella, running after it.

The ball landed in the basket and Bella dived in to get it.

'Get off!' squealed Tilly.

'Bella,' yowled the rest of the kittens, batting at her with their paws.

Bella hooked the ball out of the basket. She rolled it across the floor and skittered after it. The ball pinged off the scratching post, and into the mouth of the tunnel. The tunnel rustled noisily as Bella chased the ball and knocked it out the other end. Now where had it gone? Bella jumped out of the tunnel in time to see the ball careering across the room. Chasing after it, she swished it with a paw. The ball spun across the room, bounced off a shoe and landed in the water bowl, splashing Pixie.

'Bella!' he
growled, his
whiskers
twitching angrily.
'Go and play
somewhere
else.'

The ball bobbed in the water bowl. Bella hesitated. She didn't like getting her paws wet. Reluctantly she left the ball where it was and went to sit by the door, fixing it with her bright green eyes as if staring at it would make it open. She sat there for ages until at last her efforts were rewarded. Slowly the door swung wide.

Bella jumped up but as she tried to go through the gap, a hand pushed her gently back.

'No, little one. I'm not here to let you out. I've come to clean the room.'

'Please?' Bella pleaded.

'I know,' said the maid, totally misunderstanding her cries. 'I don't know how I'm supposed to clean with so many kittens in here either.'

Sighing heavily, the maid began lifting her cleaning equipment into the room. Bella waited until her back was turned, then slipped into the corridor. This time Bella didn't stop to work out which way Katie had gone. She scampered off before the maid could notice her escaping.

After a while, the carpet ended and large tiles covered the floor. Bella didn't like the tiles. Her paws slipped on them and she had to slow down.

There were lots of doors. Most of them were shut and Bella wondered what was inside the rooms. Then a delicious smell wafted towards her. Bella's nose twitched and her stomach grumbled hungrily. Breakfast had been a long while ago. Eagerly, she followed the lovely smell.

Her search took her to a room at the end of the corridor. There was a lot of noise coming from it but the smell was so wonderful, Bella forgot to be scared. She slipped inside and found the room full of people dressed in white hats and large aprons. It was very hot and everyone was red in the face. Bella's paws twitched with excitement. There was so much food here. A pair of legs strode towards her. Quickly Bella hid under a table. As she watched the activity, she smelt something particularly delicious.

Fish.

Bella swished her tail. Half closing her eyes, she worked out that the fish was on the counter where a lady was working. The lady had a kind face and Bella was about to ask her for a scrap of fish when the lady was called away.

'Whiskers!' Now she would have to wait.

Bella curled her black tail neatly round her white paws and stared at the counter. She waited for ages. At last she couldn't bear it any longer. Silently, she crept from under the table. The counter was too high to reach

but there was a bin next to it. Stretching up, she rested her front paws on the lid and pulled herself on top. That was easy, but the counter was still too high to reach.

Bella looked around. That nearby chair would do! Taking a deep breath, she bunched her body and sprung, landing on the seat. Bella dug her claws in to stop herself from sliding off. She reached up and put her front paws on the counter. It was hard and slippery but the fishy smell was driving her crazy.

Slowly Bella pulled herself up. Her nose

was level with the counter top when her paws began to slip. Bella stuck out her claws but it was no use – she couldn't get a good grip. In a rush of air she fell. Instinctively she twisted her body and somehow landed on her front paws. Then her bottom caught up, flipping her head over heels. Bella rolled across the floor until she bumped into a pair of shiny black shoes.

'What . . .' cried a man's voice.

There was an almighty crash as he tripped over Bella. Several louder crashes quickly followed and lots of angry voices. Bella curled into a ball, keeping her eyes tightly shut. The banging and crashing was frightening. It went on for ages but at last it stopped. Bella timidly uncurled and looked around. The shiny kitchen was now in a terrible mess.

'Whiskers!' she squeaked. 'Whose fault was that?'

Chapter 4

Bella in Trouble

Princess Katie threw open her bedroom door and pirouetted across the room. Her dance lesson had gone really well and Madame Quickstep was pleased with her. If she could dance like that at the birthday ball, Mum and Dad would be happy too. Cheerfully, Katie danced into her dressing room and wriggled out of her dancing dress.

'What shall I wear?' she said to herself.

Princess Katie had lots of pretty clothes but there was no point dressing up when she was going to play with the kittens.

'I know,' she said, picking up an old blue T-shirt with a picture of a horse on. She matched it with faded jeans with daisies on the pockets.

Katie couldn't wait to play with the kittens, especially Bella, who was such fun. Shoving her feet into a pair of trainers she went to see if Becky was back from the shops. The girls met downstairs.

'Did you get a dress?' asked Katie.

'Yes,' said Becky, her brown eyes shining. 'It's silver and blue.'

'It sounds lovely.' Katie had just opened the boot room door when an enormous crash came from further along the corridor. Silence followed, then there were more crashes and lots of shouting.

Katie's heart sank to her trainers. She had a bad feeling about the noise. She quickly did a kitten count.

'Five,' she said. 'Who's missing?'

'Bella!' Katie and Becky spoke together.

Wordlessly the girls followed the noise until they arrived at the kitchen. It was in chaos! Saucepans and smashed plates littered the floor. There was a puddle of chocolate sauce and a trail of icing. A maid sat in the middle of it all with a lap full of squashed strawberries. Other kitchen staff were running around, bumping into each other and making more mess as they chased after a small fluffy kitten.

'Oh Bella!' gasped Katie.

Bella's black and white fur stood upright and her tail was as straight and stiff as a broomstick. Her green eyes were wide with terror as she darted about the room. One of the cooks almost caught her but Bella changed direction and collided with a chef who was putting a huge cake into a cupboard, out of harm's way.

The chef lost his balance. Holding tightly to the cake he tried to right himself. Then a maid slipped in the chocolate sauce and crashed into him.

'Help!' shouted the chef, toppling forward.
Katie felt like she was watching every-

thing in slow motion. The chef raised his
hands, which were holding the cake, but as
he hit the ground he dropped it. The cake
flew through the air.

'Quick!' Becky dashed forward.

Katie snapped into action but neither she
nor Becky was fast enough. The cake hit the

floor and exploded. Sponge and icing flew
in all directions and a splodge of jam landed
on the chef's head.

Katie's chest felt so tight she could hardly breathe. The cake was ruined. Something nudged at her leg. Katie looked down and saw it was Bella leaning against her as she cleaned icing from her whiskers.

'Oh Bella!' Bending down Katie scooped the kitten into her arms. 'We're in BIG trouble now.'

Bella nuzzled her face against Katie's cheek. She was trembling and her ears were flat back.

'It's OK,' said Katie softly. 'You're safe here.'

Katie and Becky stroked her head. Bella began to relax and pushed her head against their hands.

The head cook came over. She was red in the face and she was shaking.

'Ruined!' she moaned. 'It took days to make that cake. And look at the state of my beautiful kitchen!'

'I'm sorry,' said Katie, blinking back tears. 'We'll help clear it up, won't we, Becky?'

The cook shook her head. 'The mess isn't the biggest problem. That was the queen's birthday cake! How are we going to replace it in time? Just go, Princess, and take that kitten with you.'

What if the head cook couldn't make another cake? The ball would be ruined. Her mum would be so upset and Dad would be furious. Back in the boot room she sat down with Bella in her lap.

'Listen, Bella, Dad's going to be very angry when he finds out what you've done. You've got to behave or he might send you away.'

Becky went white. 'He wouldn't do that!'

'He might,' said Katie sadly. 'He wants Mum to have the best birthday ball ever.'

'It's not Bella's fault. She's got too much energy. We need to tire her out more,' said Becky. 'If we play lots of exciting games with her then she'll sleep more and not get into so much mischief.'

'That's a great idea,' said Katie.

Katie looked at the collection of cat toys thoughtfully.

'Let's build an obstacle course. She'd love it and it would wear her out! But first I have to go and see Dad. If I tell him what happened and how we're going to keep Bella busy he might not be so cross.'

'I'll come with you,' Becky offered.

'Thanks,' said Katie, gratefully, 'but this is something I have to do on my own.'

The king was furious. At first, he wanted to give Bella away.

'Look at all the trouble she's caused. Everyone's working so hard. It's not fair to have their efforts spoilt by a naughty kitten.'

Katie clenched her hands together. Swallowing back the tears she said, 'Please, Dad, give her another chance.'

The king sighed. 'One more chance,' he said at last.

'Thank you!' Katie flung her arms round his neck.

Promising to keep an extra special eye on

Bella in future, she ran back to the boot room to tell Becky the good news.

'Phew!' said Becky. 'Let's start wearing Bella out, then.'

Bella and the other kittens watched curiously while Katie and Becky put together an obstacle course. It started with a tunnel for Bella to crawl through. At the end of the tunnel she had to chase the jingly mouse.

'Next we'll lead her over to the scratching post,' said Becky.

Katie found an old
shoe box and put it
by the scratching post
so that Bella could
reach the platform.
She placed a fishy cat treat on the top to
tempt the kitten up there, and Becky put a
cushion on the other side for her to jump
down onto. Next Bella would bat the ball
over to another tunnel made by pushing
two chairs together.

'And we'll finish by getting her to weave
between the wellington boots,' said Katie.
She arranged the collection of wellies in a
long line, putting cat treats between them to
show Bella the way.

'It looks great fun,' said Becky. 'I'd love to
try it out.'

'You're too big for the cat tunnel. And I'd like to see you sitting on top of the scratching post!' giggled Katie.

Katie picked up Bella and put her at the start. At first she tried to eat the cat treats without going round the course.

Katie and Becky patiently kept taking

her back to the beginning of the tunnel until at last she got the hang of it. Pixie wanted a turn too. Then Poppy hid under the chairs and pounced on Bella as she crawled under them. The two kittens rolled about until Pixie jumped on them both. Soon all six kittens were play fighting, chasing each other around the obstacle course and the room. Katie and Becky couldn't stop laughing.

'Did you see that?' Katie chuckled. She was laughing so hard she could hardly speak. 'Pixie was sitting on top of the scratching post batting everyone below and then he fell off.'

'Poppy was funny too,' giggled Becky. 'She batted the ball and accidentally flipped it over her head. She nearly fell over trying to see where it had gone.'

A long while later, the kittens began to tire. One by one, they flopped down in their basket. Bella was the last to stop playing. Sleepily, she climbed in the basket, squeezing in between Pixie and Poppy.

'That worked then,' said Becky.

'Yes,' said Katie. 'There's just one problem.'

'What's that?'

'The mess!' said Katie, eyeing the room.

While she and Becky were tidying, Katie wondered how things were going in the kitchen. The cook was very good at producing food at short notice, but the queen's birthday ball was in three days. Could she bake and ice a new birthday cake by then?

Chapter 5

Fun in the Barn

Early the next day, Princess Katie and Becky took the kittens down to the barn to play, carrying the kittens in a large cardboard box.

The kittens weren't keen on being shut in. They mewed loudly and wriggled about and it was awkward holding them. At the entrance to the maze, Katie and Becky stopped for a rest, sitting on a bench with the box between them. A peacock strutted over, neck stretched, his head on one side. His magnificent tail was closed and it brushed along the ground. Curiously, he eyed the box.

'If you show us your lovely tail, we'll show you what's in the box,' joked Becky.

The peacock
fixed Becky
with a steely
eye.

'He didn't
think much of
that idea,' said
Katie, with a giggle.

A scuffling noise caught her attention. A

white paw poked between the flaps of the cardboard box.

'Bella!' squeaked Katie. 'You're too good at escaping!'

Reaching into the box, she lifted Bella out and held her up to the peacock. The animals stared at each other for a second, then Bella hissed. The peacock drew back and stalked away.

'That wasn't very nice,' scolded Katie.

Bella stiffened then suddenly tried to wriggle free.

'Oh no you don't!' said Katie, following her line of gaze to a red squirrel at the base of the tree.

Hurriedly she put Bella back in the box saying, 'You can play when we get to the barn.

Bella hated riding in the box that smelt of cardboard. She didn't mind the dark but she

didn't like not being able to see where she was
going. The moment Katie opened the lid, she
jumped out. Then, remembering what Mum
had told her a long time ago, she looked
around, checking out her surroundings.

'Purrip,' squeaked Bella, recognising the
barn. This was a safe place.

Whiskers twitching, she stalked around,
taking in all the exciting smells.

Katie and Becky got busy dragging hay
bales around. Bella went over to see what
they were doing.

'Out of the way, Bella,' said Katie, gently
moving her.

Katie had soft hands and a kind voice. But
best of all she knew just where Bella liked to
be scratched. Bella nudged Katie with her
head, purring ecstatically when she rubbed

her under the
chin. Each
time Katie
stopped
scratching,
Bella butted
her hand.

'You're
funny,' Katie
giggled, sitting
her on a hay bale.

It didn't take long for Bella to guess what
Katie and Becky were doing. They were
building her another obstacle course! She
could hardly wait and wanted to help but
every time she tried, someone picked her up
and put her back on the hay bale. Bella's tail
twitched with frustration until, at last, the

course was finished. Katie carried her to the start, then Becky showed her which way to go by waving a long stick with ribbons attached.

Bella couldn't decide which was more fun – chasing the ribbons or scrambling over the obstacle course. Her brothers and sisters loved it all too. Pebbles turned it into a race. He and Bella hared round, scrambling over hay bales and crawling through the tunnels. When the kittens began to tire, Bella started a game of hide and seek. She was very good at hiding, jumping on the other kittens when they least expected it.

Long after the other kittens had collapsed in a heap, Bella was still playing. She was disappointed when Katie began to dismantle the obstacle course and put the kittens back in their box.

At last, Katie picked Bella up and hugged

her. Bella loved being held. Princess Katie was soft and warm and she could hear her heart thumping. She stared up, her green eyes wide and pleading.

'Play with me,' she purred.

But Katie lowered her into the box,

holding her tighter when she tried to wriggle free. Bella was cross at being back in the dark with the others.

'Why can't we stay here?' she complained, when the box began to move.

'We don't live here. Our basket is in the boot room,' said Pixie, reasonably.

'Stupid boot room,' grumbled Bella. Starlight Palace was such an amazing place, she wanted to be allowed to go wherever she liked. Well, she wouldn't stay put. She was getting good at finding ways out. Settling down in the box, Bella began to plot her next adventure.

It turned out to be much easier than Bella could have hoped. Not long after Katie and Becky had returned the kittens to the boot room, firmly closing the door behind them, Alfie came in.

'I'm bored!' he sighed. 'Everyone's too busy with the silly birthday ball to play with me. But you'll play with me, won't you?'

Alfie picked up the jingly mouse and waved it under Bella's nose. At once she pounced, giving chase as Alfie ran across the room. It was such fun and Bella was very disappointed when the queen came to tell Alfie he was late for his music lesson.

'See you soon!' Alfie called to the kittens,

rushing out and forgetting to close the door again.

'Who wants to explore?' Bella called to her brothers and sisters.

'Me!' squeaked everyone.

Bella's paws tingled with excitement as the other five kittens joined her outside the room.

'Which way?' asked Poppy.

Bella stared around. The kitchen was that way. As delicious as it smelt she wasn't keen on going there again. It had been much too scary.

'This way!' she said, setting out in the opposite direction.

Chapter 6

Missing Again!

'Stop!' called Madame Quickstep, clapping her hands together.

Katie landed awkwardly, flinging out her arms to balance herself.

'Do that again, from the glissade. And stop holding your head as if you're carrying china on it!' scolded Madame Quickstep.

'The tiara is *not* going to fall off.'

Katie bit back a scowl. It was all very well for Madame Quickstep to be cross, but Katie had never worn the queen's tiara before and it felt weird. It was silver, with three points that each had a silver star on top. There was a huge purple amethyst in the middle, and

pink and white diamonds studded around the sides. It was much bigger and heavier than the tiara she normally danced in and she kept thinking it was going to slide over her nose.

Forcing herself to smile politely, Katie nodded at the pianist to show she was ready, then set off across the floor. She desperately wanted to touch the tiara to check it was still in place but instead she kept her hands where they should be, letting her feet carry her to the final part of the dance. This was the tricky bit – *run, leap and fly.* Katie landed with her feet neatly together, twirled a pirouette and finished with her hands in the air.

'Bravo!' cheered Madame Quickstep. 'That was excellent. Tomorrow, come to my lesson wearing your new dress and silver shoes. You'd better practise dancing in them too.'

'I will. See you tomorrow, Madame!' Pulling the tiara off, Katie smiled with relief.

'I'll go and ask Mrs Snippet if my dress is ready,' she said to herself when she had changed out of her dancing clothes.

She went along to the sewing room and knocked on the door.

'Come in,' called Mrs Snippet. 'Hello, Princess, this is a nice surprise.'

'Hello,' said Katie, stepping into the room. 'Is that Mum's dress you're working on?'

'Yes. I'm almost finished. I've been sewing lace around the hem. It's taken me ages. What do you think?'

Mrs Snippet held up the skirt of the queen's dress for Katie to see.

'Oh,' said Katie, smiling to cover her dismay.

The lace was nice but a bit old fashioned. The dress had looked much prettier without it. 'I . . . It . . . I think it's lovely,' she said bravely.

'Me too,' sighed Mrs Snippet. 'It's the perfect finishing touch.'

'I wondered if my dress was finished?' asked Katie, quickly changing the subject. 'Madame Quickstep wants me to practise dancing in it.'

'Sorry, Princess, but I've been working on this all day. I'll start on your dress first thing tomorrow.'

'Thank you.' Swallowing her disappointment, Katie left Mrs Snippet to her work. It was her last dance lesson tomorrow and the queen's birthday ball the day after. Trying not to worry that she would have no time to practise dancing in her dress, Katie went to give the kittens their tea. She was surprised to find the boot room door open. Her heart sank as she entered the room. It was empty. The kittens had escaped!

'No,' she groaned, covering her face with her hands.

Dashing into the hallway Katie ran head first into Alfie.

'Hi,' he said cheerfully. 'I've come to see the kittens again.'

Katie's eyes narrowed suspiciously. '*Again?*'

'Yes,' said Alfie.

'Alfie! You left the door open and the kittens have escaped.'

'I didn't,' he argued.

'You must have.'

Alfie stamped his foot. 'Didn't.'

'What's going on?' asked Becky, arriving. 'Why are you arguing?'

'The kittens have escaped,' said Katie. Turning to Alfie she added crossly, '*Someone* forgot to shut the door!'

'We'd better find them before they get into trouble,' said Becky, sensibly. 'You go this way, Katie. Alfie, you go that way and I'll look in the kitchens.'

Katie felt suddenly sick. What if Bella was in the kitchens again? There wasn't time to start on yet another birthday cake. The ball would be ruined and Bella would definitely be sent away.

'I've got a better idea,' said Alfie suddenly.

'It's nearly teatime isn't it? Wait here a minute.'

He ran off and returned carrying a metal feeding bowl and a fork. 'Watch this,' he said.

Banging the fork against the bowl, he yelled, 'Here, kitties, time for tea!'

Katie and Becky jumped in surprise and covered their ears with their hands as Alfie continued to beat on the bowl.

Sure enough, a few seconds later, Pixie appeared with Poppy trotting after him.

'Wow! That's brilliant, Alfie,' said Katie, impressed with his quick-thinking.

Katie and Becky ushered the kittens into the boot room. Pebbles and Tilly came next and a few minutes later the white kitten, Suki. She raced towards them and nearly fell head over heels as she skidded into the boot room.

'Careful!' said Katie, bending down to steady her.

'Three ... four ... five,' counted Becky. 'So who's missing?'

'Bella!' chorused everyone.

Alfie continued banging the food bowl but either Bella couldn't hear it or she was choosing to ignore the summons.

'Alfie, can you be very grown up and feed the kittens while we go and find Bella? They have a third of a tin of kitten food each. You have to watch to make sure they don't eat each other's, and they need fresh water,' Katie asked.

Alfie went pink with pleasure. 'Of course I can do it!' he said.

Katie's heart banged loudly as she and Becky began their search. Where had Bella gone *this* time?

Bella was having fun. Starlight Palace was enormous, with lots of different and exciting rooms to explore. She rolled on thick carpets, played pouncing games with patches of sunlight, hid under chairs and climbed up some curtains. The curtains had a lovely velvety feel, but when she was halfway up, they began to swing. Alarmed, Bella dug her claws in harder. Gradually the curtains slowed until Bella decided it was safe to get down. But now one of her claws was stuck.

She tried to pull herself free but that made the curtain sway faster again. Bella's fur fluffed out in alarm. Desperate to get back to the ground, she yanked her paw away as hard as she could. There was a funny ripping sound. A small strand of red velvet was stuck in her claw but at least she was free. Hurriedly, she scrambled to the floor and nibbled the velvet free as she sat behind the curtain.

Ready to go exploring again, Bella went out of the room and found a staircase which twirled upwards. It was great fun to climb and led to lots more exciting rooms, one full of toys. There were cuddly animals and a wooden castle and a train set, but Bella loved the car best. It was big enough for her to sit on, and, by running at the car and jumping on top of it, Bella got a ride. Soon she'd invented a new game, seeing how far she could get the car to zoom across the floor.

A long while later, Bella had finally had enough of playing with the toys. She was tired, her paws ached and she longed for a cuddle. She padded along the hallway looking for Katie, Becky or her new friend Alfie. Bella nosed open a door. Was Katie in here? Bella hoped so. The room looked familiar – it was the one with the dummies dressed up in clothes. Katie had been here once, so maybe she'd come again.

Bella crawled hopefully under the long white sheet to wait for her. Underneath, she was surprised to find the silky dress now had some pretty lacy stuff at the bottom. Bella kneaded the material with her paws. It felt wonderful! When she was comfortable she settled down with her face pressed against it.

Sleepily, she closed her eyes. She half heard someone enter the room and a little while later the click of a door, but she was too tired to go and investigate.

Ages later, Bella woke up. Yawning lazily, she stretched out her paws. Her tummy growled emptily – it must be teatime. Bella stood up, but the lacy fabric stuck to her claws. Each time she yanked a paw free, there was a funny ripping sound. It reminded Bella of the velvet curtains, only the ripping lace felt much nicer. Bella rolled around, fighting the lace, loving the sound and feel of it as it tore, until her stomach growled again. Remembering it was teatime, she finally freed her claws and nosed her way from under the dress and sheet. The room was in semi darkness but Bella could see well and made her way to the door.

To her dismay, it was shut. Bella scratched it with her claws. That didn't help. She jumped for the door handle but it was far too high for her to reach. Desperate to get out, Bella kept clawing at the door. But it was no use. Bella's heart thudded uncomfortably as she realised she was trapped.

Chapter 7

Ruined!

'Where's Bella?' asked Katie, for the umpteenth time.

The queen perched on the edge of Katie's bed. 'She'll be in the palace somewhere,' she said reassuringly.

'But what if she's causing trouble?' wailed Katie.

'Bella will be fine,' said the queen, smoothing Katie's duvet. 'You tired her out today so I expect she's curled up somewhere fast asleep. Stop worrying and get some rest. You've got a busy couple of days coming up.'

Katie sighed as she settled down. But long after Mum had hugged her goodnight she was still wide awake and worrying about Bella. The nights were still quite cold. What if the kitten had strayed outside? Or worse still, what if she wasn't tired and was causing damage somewhere? According to Becky, the new birthday cake had been made and was waiting to be iced. What if Bella got into the kitchen and wrecked it?

Katie drifted into a restless sleep and woke very early next morning. Unable to stay in bed, she got up and immediately went to look for Bella. She started at the boot room in case the little kitten had somehow found her way back there. Instead she found Becky, peering at the five sleeping kittens.

'What are you doing here?' asked Katie in surprise.

'Same as you,' Becky sighed. 'I didn't sleep a wink last night worrying about Bella. I even got Mum to go and check the kitchens for me, but luckily Bella wasn't there.'

Quietly the girls searched the palace. They weren't the only ones up so early. There were lots of people hard at work preparing for the queen's birthday ball, putting up sparkling decorations, arranging wonderfully scented flowers, practising music and stringing up fairy lights. Katie and Becky kept out of their way as they searched the ground floor then took the lift to the first. As the lift doors slid open, there was a shrill scream. Katie went ice cold. She recognised that voice. Fearfully, she and Becky ran to the sewing room where Mrs Snippet was in a flood of tears.

'What's wrong?' asked Katie, giving her a hug.

'It's ruined!' sobbed the dressmaker. 'The queen's dress is ruined. Th–th–that naughty kitten ripped all the lace.'

Katie's chest was so tight she could hardly breathe as Mrs Snippet held out the spoilt dress. From the corner of her eye she could see Bella cowering in the corner. Katie's relief at finding the kitten was replaced with a sick fear. If Mum's dress was ruined, then so was the birthday ball!

'Torn and covered in cat hair,' moaned Mrs Snippet, putting her face in her hands.

'Can I have a look?' asked Becky. Stepping forward she took a long look at the dress.

'It's not as bad as you think,' she said at last. 'Mum has a special clothes brush that will get rid of the cat hair. And it's only the lace hem that's torn. Not the dress. If you took it off really carefully, I don't think any one would know.'

Katie felt a tiny spark of hope. 'The dress did look lovely without the lace,' she said.

Mrs Snippet dried her eyes. While she examined the dress, Katie picked up Bella. She was trembling with fright and Katie stroked the kitten's head to calm her down.

As Bella relaxed she snuggled into Katie's chest.

'Oh Bella, you've really done it this time,' whispered Katie, sadly. If Mrs Snippet couldn't mend Mum's dress, Bella would surely have to go.

'Well,' said Mrs Snippet, at last. 'I'm not sure I can take the lace off without making holes in the material but I'll have a go. It's going to take ages to remake the hem though and I've still got *your* dress to finish off. Let's hope I get everything done in time.'

★ 🐾 ★

Princess Katie was so worried about her mother's dress that she did badly in her last dance lesson. Madame Quickstep shook her head with disappointment.

'I'm very sorry, Princess, but after that performance I don't think I can let you dance at the ball.'

Katie gasped. '*Please* let me,' she pleaded. 'I won't go riding. I'll stay here and practise instead.'

Madame Quickstep sighed. 'Very well. But only if you promise to concentrate!'

Katie was sad to miss her riding lesson but the dance was more important. By the end of the day she was exhausted and close to tears, especially when she learnt that the

queen's dress *still* wasn't finished. It was a much bigger job than Mrs Snippet had realised and now she'd run out of thread.

She'd ordered more by special delivery, but the thread was coming from a long way away. Kind Mrs Snippet offered to stay in the palace overnight so that she'd be ready to start work the moment the thread arrived.

Princess Katie had another night sleepless with worry. The birthday cake was finished, but what about the dresses? The following morning she was so tired it was a struggle to get out of bed. But there wasn't time to lie in. It was Mum's birthday and tonight there would be a grand ball in her honour. If she had a dress! Shoving her arms into her dressing gown, Katie ran along to Mrs Snippet's room to see if the thread had arrived.

Chapter 8

Clever Alfie

Princess Katie stood in the middle of the packed ballroom, feet together, head up. It was so quiet you could have heard a mouse squeak. Nervously, she looked around at the sea of people waiting for her to dance. They were wearing the most amazing clothes and jewellery.

But the queen looked the best of all, dressed in her beautiful blue ball gown, stitched with tiny silk flowers from the shoulder to the hem. Mrs Snippet had done an amazing job. No one would ever guess that the dress had been damaged.

Katie was very conscious of her own ball gown. There had not been time to practice in it. It felt stiff and unfamiliar. Would she be able to dance in it? After everything that had happened it would be awful if she ruined the ball by dancing badly, it was only just ready in time for the ball. Her heart fluttered wildly until she remembered Madame Quickstep's advice.

Don't think about the dress. Take deep breaths and concentrate on the dance.

Katie breathed in deeply and started to feel

better. She nodded to the pianist, counting herself in as the music started. Slowly she raised her arms, took three steps forward, turned and jumped. The dress caught round her legs and she wobbled slightly on the point. Gathering herself together, she danced across the floor, but now she was on the wrong leg for the next jump.

Concentrate! she scolded herself.

As Katie came out of the jump, she almost fell over with surprise. What was Alfie doing under that table? Her eyes wanted to follow him but she forced herself to ignore her naughty little brother. As she turned again, she caught another glimpse of him. He had one hand clutched to his chest as he slowly crawled along. Katie blinked and forced the picture out of her mind. She was determined not to let Alfie spoil her dance. She was getting used to the feel of her dress but the tricky part was still to come.

Katie's silver shoes sparkled as she leapt into the air, her lilac and pink skirts billowing as she finished with a pirouette. Hands above her head she held the pose then slowly curtsied to her audience.

The room fell silent. Katie looked for Mum. There she was, right at the front, looking beautiful and smiling proudly. The queen blew her a kiss and Katie blew one back.

'Bravo,' called the king, clapping loudly.

The guests clapped too, cheering and calling for an encore. Katie was relieved when Madame Quickstep appeared by her side to lead her off. She'd really enjoyed dancing but she couldn't face doing it all over again.

Katie hardly heard Madame Quickstep telling her how well she'd performed. She was too cross with Alfie.

Dad patted her arm, then Mum hugged her saying, 'Thank you, darling! That was brilliant. This is my BEST birthday ball ever!'

Katie forced a smile. It was a good thing they hadn't seen Alfie. Whatever was he up to? She had to find out before he ruined the evening.

The king and queen returned to their guests and Katie found Becky and told her what she'd seen.

'Ball gowns weren't meant for running in,' said Becky, holding up her silver and blue skirt as she hurried from the ballroom.

'You should try dancing in one!' Katie exclaimed.

The long corridor outside was empty.

'Where's Alfie gone?' said Becky, staring up and down.

'He's *such* a pain. He's almost as bad as Bella sometimes,' sighed Katie.

Suddenly Katie and Becky stared at each other.

'Bella!' they exclaimed.

'NO!' gasped Becky, her eyes wide. 'Surely she didn't . . .'

'It would be just like her,' said Katie.

Together they tore along to the boot room. There was a lot of noise coming from inside. Katie opened the door and found Alfie rolling on the floor, in his new green velvet suit, teasing Bella with the jingly mouse. He sat up guiltily.

'Sorry, Katie, I missed your dance. I heard

the clapping though, so it must have been good.'

'*I* saw *you* though,' said Katie. 'You were under a table!'

Alfie turned bright red. 'Did anyone else see me?'

'No,' said Becky, a smile creeping to her

lips. 'It was Bella's fault wasn't it?'

Alfie nodded. 'She escaped again. It was lucky I saw her. She was climbing up to the food table to get at the prawns!'

'So you caught her and brought her back here?' asked Katie.

Alfie nodded. 'I really wanted to see your dance but I thought I'd better play with Bella in case she tried to escape again.'

'Oh wow!' said Becky. 'Clever Alfie, he's a little brother in a million!'

Alfie turned even redder.

Katie blushed too, guiltily remembering how she thought Alfie was being naughty. Thinking hard, she tapped the carpet with one silver foot.

'I love all my kittens,' she said slowly, 'but I don't have enough time to look after Bella.

She's the sort of cat that needs one owner to give her lots of attention. Alfie, would you like to have Bella? She can still live here with the other kittens but I'm sure she wouldn't get into anywhere near as much trouble if you were looking after her.'

'Really?'

Alfie picked Bella up and hugged her to him. 'Did you hear that, Bella? You're my cat now.'

'Is that a yes?' asked Katie with a grin.

'YES!' yelled Alfie. 'Thank you, Katie, you're the best sister ever! And Bella's the best kitten. Are you sure you won't miss her?'

Katie looked at the other five kittens squashed together in their basket.

'A little, but I'll still see her every day and the others will keep us busy, won't they, Becky?'

Becky smiled. 'I think they will!'

Princess Katie's Kittens

Collect all the kittens!

Pixie
at the Palace

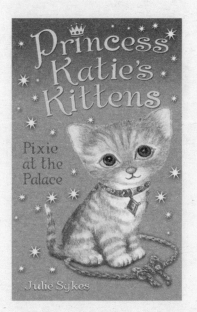

One of the newly found kittens has gone missing in the woods. Can Princess Katie and her best friend Becky find Pixie and bring him safely back to Starlight Palace?

★ Coming soon ★

Poppy
and the Prince

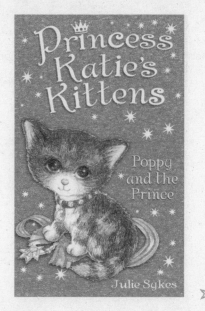

Poppy tries to make friends with Prince
Edward, who thinks cats are silly – but
when the prince gets lost in the palace
maze, it's Poppy who saves the day!

★ Coming soon ★

Suki in the Snow

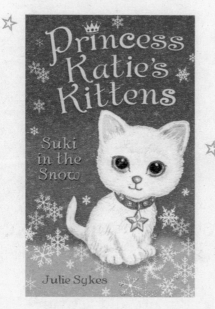

Suki has crept into Princess Katie's luggage and has come on her skiing holiday! But when Suki tries to make her own way home, Katie and Becky race against time to find the kitten lost in the snow.

Princess Katie's Kittens

PrincessKatiesKittens.co.uk

Meet all the kittens

Puzzles and activities

How to care for kittens

Competitions

Book news and more!